# The
# Language of
# Happiness

Other books by

# Blue Mountain Press INC.

# The Language of Happiness

Edited by Susan Polis Schutz

Designed and Illustrated
by Stephen Schutz

**Blue Mountain Press** ™

Boulder, Colorado

Library of Congress Number: 77-93903
ISBN: 0-88396-026-5

Manufactured in the United States of America

First Printing: June, 1978
Second Printing: November, 1978
Third Printing: May, 1979

**Blue Mountain Press** INC.

P.O. Box 4549, Boulder, Colorado 80306

## ACKNOWLEDGMENTS

Hoyt Axton for "I feel we could be happy," by Hoyt Axton. From the song ON THE
NATURAL. Copyright © 1968, 1972 Lady Jane Music. International Copyright Secured. All
rights reserved. Used by permission.

Robert L. Bell for "Happiness," by Max Ehrmann. Copyright © 1948 by Bertha K. Ehrmann.
All rights reserved. Reprinted by permission Robert L. Bell, Melrose, Massachusetts 02176.

Peter McWilliams for "I love you," by Peter McWilliams. From the book I LOVE THERE-
FORE I AM, published by Leo Press, 5806 Elizabeth Court, Allen Park, MI 48101. Copyright
© 1970, 1972 by Peter McWilliams. All rights reserved. Used by permission.

Harold Ober Associates Incorporated for "I could not be," by Woodrow Wilson. From the
book THE PRICELESS GIFT, published by Alfred A. Knopf, Inc. Copyright © 1962 by
Eleanor Wilson McAdoo. All rights reserved. And for "Hold fast to dreams," by Langston
Hughes. From the book THE DREAM KEEPER. Copyright © 1932 by Alfred A. Knopf, Inc.
Renewed Copyright © 1960 by Langston Hughes. Reprinted by permission of Harold Ober
Associates Incorporated.

Warner Bros., Inc. for "The fire is dying now," by Gordon Lightfoot. From the song
SONG FOR A WINTER'S NIGHT. Copyright © 1965 Warner Bros., Inc. All rights
reserved. Reprinted by permission.

The following works have previously appeared in Blue Mountain Press publications:

"Can you have hope?" by David Polis. Copyright © Continental Publications, 1974. All rights
reserved.
"I sit here bored," by Susan Polis Schutz. Copyright © Continental Publications, 1973. All
rights reserved.
"Sounds of the wind," by June Polis. Copyright © Continental Publications, 1971. All rights
reserved.
"You taught me," by Susan Polis Schutz. Copyright © Continental Publications, 1976. All
rights reserved.

A careful effort has been made to trace the ownership of poems used in this anthology in
order to get permission to reprint copyrighted poems and to give proper credit to the copyright owners.

If any error or omission has occurred, it is completely inadvertent, and we would like to
correct it in future editions provided that written notification is made to the publisher:
BLUE MOUNTAIN PRESS, INC., P.O. Box 4549, Boulder, Colorado 80306

# CONTENTS

$T$he best and most beautiful
things in the world
cannot be seen
or even touched.
They must be felt
with the heart

Helen Keller

**H**appiness cannot come from without.
It must come from within. It is not what we
see and touch or that which others do for us
which makes us happy; it is that which
we think and feel and do, first for the other
fellow and then for ourselves

Helen Keller

# IT'S YOU THAT MAKES ME HAPPY

The fire is dying now,
my lamp is growing dim,
the shades of night
are lifting.
The morning light steals
across my window pane,
where webs of snow
are drifting.
If I could only
have you near . . .
I would be happy
just . . . to be once
again with you

Gordon Lightfoot

**I** love you
   for the love you give me.

You love me
for the love I give you.

I do not know who first gave
or who first took
or where it all began

But I am happy that it did.

I am happy that it is.

I am happy as it is.

I am in short
     in long
     in love
      (and happy!)

Peter McWilliams

# IT'S YOU THAT MAKES ME HAPPY

**Y**ou taught me to appreciate nature
the day we picked mint leaves
                    in the mountains
You taught me honesty
the night I saw tears in your eyes
You taught me to dream
the first time we were apart from
                        each other
You taught me to feel
when I discovered love
You taught me happiness
when I discovered you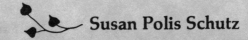

Susan Polis Schutz

## IT'S YOU THAT MAKES ME HAPPY

To love is to place our happiness in the happiness of another

 Leibnitz

Love, and love alone, is capable of giving thee a happier life

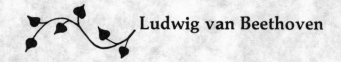 Ludwig van Beethoven

**I** could not be what I am, if I did not take such serene happiness from my union with you. You are my spring of content; and so long as I have you, and you too are happy, nothing but good and power can come to me . . . may God bless and keep you!

Woodrow Wilson

## IT'S YOU THAT MAKES ME HAPPY

**I** wish you all the good and charm that
life can offer. Think of me kindly, and . . .
rest assured that no one would more
rejoice to hear of your happiness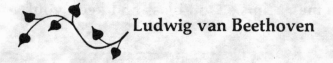

Ludwig van Beethoven

**I** sit here
bored
I don't feel like talking
to the people here
I don't feel like looking
at this place anymore

I sit here
lonely
realizing that it's not
people or places that
make me happy
It's you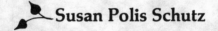

— Susan Polis Schutz

# THE HAPPINESS OF HELEN KELLER

**M**any persons have a wrong idea about what constitutes true happiness. It is not attained through self-gratification, but through fidelity to a worthy purpose

Helen Keller

# Keep
your face to
the sunshine
and you cannot
see the shadow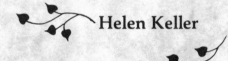

Helen Keller

# EXUBERANCE OF NATURE

I feel . . .
    we could be happy in the mountains.
Everybody's talking about the place
of their dreams,
where they can find peace of mind.
I'm not sure, but I think it seems
I've finally found mine . . .
    in the mountains 🐦🐦

Hoyt Axton

Sounds of the wind
sounds of the sea
make one happy
just to be 🐦🐦

June Polis

Joy is everywhere;
it is in the earth's
green covering of grass:
in the blue
serenity of the sky:
in the reckless
exuberance of spring:
in the severe abstinence
of grey winter:
in the living flesh
that animates our bodily frame:
in the perfect poise
of the human figure,
noble and upright:
in living, in the exercise
of all our powers:
in the acquisition of knowledge
. . . Joy is there everywhere

Rabindranath Tagore

# PHILOSOPHY OF HAPPINESS

**C**an you have hope for
tomorrow's world without
the experience of
yesterday's world?
Can you be so busy teaching
others without having time
for learning from others?
Can you have real knowledge
and also fear new ideas?
Can you really be secure
without growth, reform,
and change?
Can you count the blessings
of others and not count
your own?
Can you be happy with your
success without being
happy about the success
of others?

Can you be happy always
   "Taking" without ever
   "Giving"?
Can you say "why did this
   sorrow happen to me?"
   —when you don't say "why
   did this joy happen to me?"
Can you praise a person
   for bringing happiness into
   your life without praising
   God for his part in bringing
   that person into your life?

David Polis

# PHILOSOPHY OF HAPPINESS

I have never given very deep thought
to a philosophy of life, though I have a few
ideas that I think are useful to me.
One is that you do whatever comes your way
to do as well as you can, and another
is that you think as little as possible about
yourself and as much as possible about other
people and about things that are interesting.
The third is that you get more joy
out of giving joy to others and should
put a good deal of thought into the happiness
that you are able to give.

Eleanor Roosevelt

**B**e glad of life
because it gives
you the chance
to love and to work
and to play and to
look up at the stars

Henry van Dyke

**T**he grand essentials
to happiness
in this life are
something to do
something to love
and something
        to hope for

Joseph Addison

# THE PURSUIT OF HAPPINESS

**H**appiness is an endowment and not
an acquisition. It depends more upon
temperament and disposition than
environment. It is a state or condition of
mind, and not a commodity to be bought or
sold in the market. A beggar may be
happier in his rags than a king in his purple.
Poverty is no more incompatible with
happiness than wealth, and the inquiry,
"How to be happy though poor?" implies a
want of understanding of the conditions
upon which happiness depends. Dives
was not happy because he was a millionaire,
nor Lazarus wretched because he was a
pauper. There is a quality in the soul of man
that is superior to circumstances and that
defies calamity and misfortune. The man who
is unhappy when he is poor would be
unhappy if he were rich, and he who is

happy in a palace in Paris would be happy
in a dug-out on the frontier of Dakota.
There are as many unhappy rich men as there
are unhappy poor men. Every heart knows
its own bitterness and its own joy. Not
that wealth and what it brings is not
desirable—books, travel, leisure, comfort,
the best food and raiment, agreeable
companionship—but all these do not
necessarily bring happiness and may coexist
with the deepest wretchedness, while
adversity and penury, exile and privation are
not incompatible with the loftiest exaltation
of the soul

John J. Ingalls

# THE PURSUIT OF HAPPINESS

If you ever find happiness by hunting for it, you will find it as the old woman did her lost spectacles—on her own nose all the time ▲ ▲

Josh Billings

The great thing
in this world
is not so much
where we are,
but in what direction
we are moving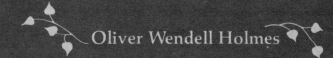

Oliver Wendell Holmes

# THE PURSUIT OF HAPPINESS

**S**ome of us might find happiness if we would
quit struggling so desperately for it

                        William Feather

**I** accept life unconditionally . . . .
Most people ask for happiness on condition.
Happiness can only be felt if you
don't set any condition

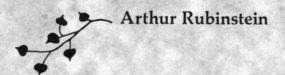

                        Arthur Rubinstein

**P**erfect happiness is the absence of the
striving for happiness; perfect renown is the
absence of concern for renown

— Chuang-Tse

**I**t was probably a mistake to pursue happiness;
much better to create happiness; still better
to create happiness for others. The more
happiness you created for others the more
would be yours—a solid satisfaction
that no one could ever take away from you

Lloyd Douglas

# HAPPY THE MAN

There are as many nights as days, and the one is just as long as the other in the year's course. Even a happy life cannot be without a measure of darkness, and the word "happiness" would lose its meaning if it were not balanced by sadness. It is far better to take things as they come along with patience and equanimity

Carl Gustav Jung

**H**appy the man
and happy he alone,
He who secure within
can say:
"Tomorrow doesn't
matter, for I have
lived today"

Horace

**I**n the midst of
winter, I finally
learned that there
was in me an
invincible summer

Albert Camus

# ENJOY YOURSELF!

**I**f we are ever to enjoy life, now is the time. Today should always be our most wonderful day

**Thomas Dreier**

**I**t is not how much we have, but how much we enjoy, that makes happiness

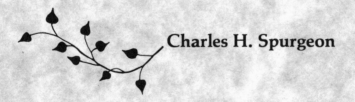

**Charles H. Spurgeon**

**I** find ecstasy in living; the mere sense of living is joy enough 🍃🍃

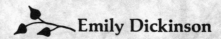Emily Dickinson

**T**o live is not merely to breathe, it is to act; it is to make use of our organs, senses, faculties, of all those parts of ourselves which give us the feeling of existence. The man who has lived longest is not the man who has counted most years, but he who has enjoyed life most 🍃🍃

Jean-Jacques Rousseau

## ENJOY YOURSELF!

Hold fast to dreams
for if dreams die,
   life is a broken
      winged bird that
         cannot fly

Langston Hughes

**S**low down and enjoy life. It's not only the scenery you miss by going too fast—
you also miss the sense of where you're going and why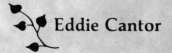

Eddie Cantor

**I** have enjoyed the happiness of the world;
I have lived and loved

Schiller

# A UNION WITH GOD

**T**he thought of God, and nothing short of it,
is the happiness of man ✿ ✿

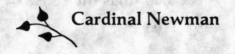

Cardinal Newman

**H**appiness is neither within us only, nor
without us; it is the union of ourselves
with God ✿ ✿

Pascal

# HAPPINESS DWELLS WITHIN

**J**oy is not in things; it is in us

Richard Wagner

**V**ery little is needed to make a happy life. It is all within yourself

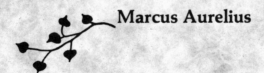

Marcus Aurelius

H appiness
resides not in
possessions and
not in gold, the
feeling of happiness
dwells in the soul

Democritus

Happiness is not in our circumstances,
but in ourselves. It is not something we see,
like a rainbow, or feel, like the heat of a fire.
Happiness is something we are

 John B. Sheerin

# WORK TOWARD HAPPINESS

**W**ho are the happiest people on earth?
A craftsman or artist whistling over a job well
done. A little child building sand castles.
A mother, after a busy day, bathing her baby.
A doctor who has finished a difficult and
dangerous operation, and saved a human life.
Happiness lies in a constructive job well done.

Get your happiness out of your work or you
will never know what happiness is

Elbert Hubbard

**T**o be without desire is to be content.
But contentment is not happiness. And in
contentment there is no progress. Happiness
is to desire something, to work for it,
and to obtain at least a part of it. In the
pursuit of beloved labor the busy days pass
cheerfully employed, and the still nights
in peaceful sleep. For labor born of desire is
not drudgery, but manly play. Success
brings hope, hope inspires fresh desire, and
desire gives zest to life and joy to labor.
This is true whether your days be spent in the
palaces of the powerful or in some little
green by-way of the world. Therefore, while
yet you have the strength, cherish a desire
to do some useful work in your little corner of
the world, and have the steadfastness to
labor. For this is the way to the happy life;
with health and endearing ties, it is the
way to the glorious life

Max Ehrmann

# WORK TOWARD HAPPINESS

## The Joy of Work

Give us, oh, give us, the man who sings at his work! He will do more in the same time —he will do it better —he will persevere longer. One is scarcely sensible of fatigue whilst he marches to music. The very stars are said to make harmony as they revolve in their spheres. Wondrous is the strength of cheerfulness, altogether past calculation in its powers of endurance. Efforts, to be permanently useful, must be uniformly joyous, a spirit all sunshine, graceful from very gladness, beautiful because bright

Thomas Carlyle

**A**ll real and wholesome enjoyments possible
to man have been just as possible to him
since he was made of the earth as they are now;
and they are possible to him chiefly in peace.
To watch the corn grow, and the blossoms
set; to draw hard breath over plowshare
or spade; to read, to think, to love, to hope,
to pray—these are the things that make
men happy

John Ruskin

# Happiness is . . .

. . . the calm, glad certainty of innocence

Henrik Ibsen

. . . the grace of being permitted to unfold . . . all the spiritual powers planted within us

Franz Werfel

. . . the conviction that we are loved . . . in spite of ourselves

Victor Hugo

. . . tranquility of mind

Cicero

. . . enjoying the realities as well as the frivolities of life

Edward G. Bulwer-Lytton

. . . made up of minute fractions . . . countless infinitesimals of pleasurable and genial feeling

Samuel Taylor Coleridge

# HAPPINESS IS . . .

. . . the meaning and the purpose of life, the whole aim and end of human existence

Aristotle

. . . living on a farm which is one's own, far from the hectic, artificial conditions of the city — a farm where one gets directly from one's own soil what one needs to sustain life, with a garden in front and a healthy, normal family to contribute those small domestic joys

Thomas Edison

. . . a butterfly, which, when pursued,
is always just beyond your grasp, but
which, if you will sit down quietly, may
alight upon you

Nathaniel Hawthorne

. . . the quality of your thoughts

Marcus Aurelius

# NONE BUT FREEDOM

**S**upreme happiness consists in self-content;
that we may gain this self-content,
we are placed upon this earth and endowed
with freedom

           Jean – Jacques Rousseau

**T**he secret of Happiness is Freedom,
and the secret of Freedom, Courage

           Thucydides

**T**he necessity of pursuing true happiness is the foundation of our liberty ᔕᔕ

John Locke

**H**uman happiness has no perfect security but freedom; freedom none but virtue; virtue none but knowledge ᔕᔕ

Josiah Quincy

## NONE BUT FREEDOM

Our greatest happiness . . . does not depend on the condition of life in which chance has placed us, but is always the result of a good conscience, good health, occupation, and freedom in all just pursuits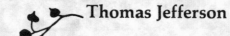

— Thomas Jefferson

Justice is the only worship. Love is the only priest. Ignorance is the only slavery. Happiness is the only good. The time to be happy is now. The place to be happy is here. The way to be happy is to make other people happy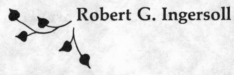

Robert G. Ingersoll

# OF HEART AND MIND

**H**appiness itself is sufficient excuse.
Beautiful things are right and true; so beautiful
actions are those pleasing to the gods.
Wise men have an inward sense of what is
beautiful, and the highest wisdom is to trust
this intuition and be guided by it. The
answer to the last appeal of what is right lies
within a man's own breast. Trust thyself 🍃🍃

Aristotle

The happiest people are those who think the most interesting thoughts. Interesting thoughts can only live in cultivated minds. Those who decide to use leisure as a means of mental development, who love good music, good books, good pictures, good plays at the theater, good company, good conversation—what are they? They are the happiest people in the world; and they are not only happy in themselves, they are the cause of happiness in others

William Lyon Phelps

# OF HEART AND MIND

**A** man's happiness and success in life will
depend not so much upon what he has,
or upon what position he occupies, as upon
what he is, and the heart he carries
into his position

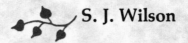

S. J. Wilson

**T**he more a man finds his sources of pleasure
in himself, the happier he will be . . .
The highest, most varied and lasting
pleasures are those of the mind

Arthur Schopenhauer

# OF HEART AND MIND

**H**appiness is not a matter of events;
it depends upon the tides of the mind

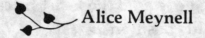 — Alice Meynell

**I** have learned too much of the vanity of
human affairs to expect any felicity
from public life. But I am determined to be
cheerful and happy in whatever situation
I may be. For I have also learned from
experience that the greater part of our
happiness or misery depends on our
dispositions and not on our circumstances

— Martha Washington

# SHARE WITH OTHERS

**H**appiness is a sunbeam which may pass
through a thousand bosoms without losing
a particle of its original ray; nay, when
it strikes on a kindred heart, like the
converged light on a mirror, it reflects
itself with redoubled brightness. It is
not perfected 'till it is shared

Jane Porter

## SHARE WITH OTHERS

**A**ll who joy would win
Must share it . . .
Happiness was born a twin

Lord Byron

**G**rief can take care of itself;
but to get the full value of a joy
you must have somebody to
divide it with

Mark Twain

**C**oming
together
is a beginning
Keeping
together
is progress
Working
together
is success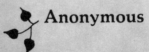

Anonymous

## COMPANIONS AND FRIENDS

**M**uch certainty of the happiness and purity
of our lives depends on our making a
wise choice of our companions and friends

John Lubbock

**T**rue happiness consists not in the multitude of friends, but in their worth and choice

 Ben Jonson

# COMPANIONS AND FRIENDS

The happiest moments my heart knows are those in which it is pouring forth its affections to a few esteemed characters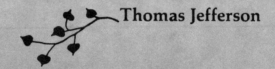

— Thomas Jefferson

**A**lways remain a faithful, good, honest friend.
That I could ever forget you, and especially
all of you who were so kind and affectionate
to me, no, do not believe it; there are
moments in which I myself long for you—
yes, and wish to spend some time with you.
—My native land, the beautiful country in
which I first saw the light of the world, is
ever as beautiful and distinct before
mine eyes as when I left you. In short, I
shall regard that time as one of the happiest
of my life, when I see you again

Ludwig van Beethoven